MR. FROG
Went a-
COURTING
Discover the Secret Story

by Gary Chalk

DORLING KINDERSLEY
LONDON • NEW YORK • STUTTGART

Mr. Frog Went a-Courting

Mr. Frog went a-court-in', he did ride, M-hm ___ M-hm

Mr. Frog went a-court-in', he did ride, A

sword and pis-tol by his side, M-hm ___ M-hm ___

Mr. Frog went a-courting, he did ride,
A sword and pistol by his side.

He rode up to Miss Mousie's door,
Where he had never been before.

He took Miss Mousie on his knee,
Said, "Miss Mouse, will you marry me?"

Now Uncle Rat when he came home,
Said, "Who's been here since I been gone?"

"A very fine gentleman has been here,
Who wishes me to be his dear."

Uncle Rat laughed and shook his sides,
To think his niece would be a bride.

Uncle Rat on a horse he went to town,
To buy his niece a wedding gown.

Where shall the wedding supper be?
Away down yonder in the hollow tree.

What shall the wedding supper be?
Three green beans and a black-eyed pea.

Tell us what was the bride dressed in?
A cream gauze veil and a brass breastpin.

Tell us what was the groom dressed in?
Sky blue breeches with silver stitches.

First to come in was a bumblebee,
To play the fiddle upon his knee.

Next to come in was a little black tick,
Ate so much it made him sick.

Next to come in was Dr. Fly,
Said Mr. Tick would surely die.

Who then came into the room,
Asked to see the bride and groom?

"Away down yonder in the hollow tree,
Who shall the wedding supper be?

I'm the famous big gray cat,
Who fancies a dinner of mouse and rat!"

He helped himself to the wedding cake,
Then chased the party down to the lake.

They all went sailing across the lake,
And they all were swallowed by a big black snake.

And there's the end of one, two, three,
The rat, the frog, and Miss Mousie!

And now begins another tale,
Of the other frog, a young female,

Who took revenge on Mr. Frog.
Will she now marry Captain Dog?

There's bread and cheese upon the shelf.
If you want any more you can sing it yourself!

ave you ever heard the story about Mr. Frog who went a-courting and married a mouse? It is a very old story and one that was sung rather than told or written down. It's always been lots of fun because people enjoyed making up their own verses about Mr. Frog, Miss Mousie, and her Uncle Rat.

Our version of the story is retold in the words of this book. But there is also another story. One that has never been told before. If you look closely at the pictures you will discover the secret tale of *Miss* Froggie, who has good reason to make sure that Mr. Frog's courtship does *not* have a happy ending.

Here are the characters you will meet in the story.

Mr. Frog – an overdressed cavalier

Miss Mousie – a spoiled mouse maiden, and Lord Rat's niece

Lord Rat – the local squire, and possessor of untold wealth

Miss Froggie – a beautiful maiden frog whose story is told in the pictures of this book, as assisted by,

Gray McMange

Captain H. Dog

Roger Rat

Ginger Tom

nce upon a time, when the world was upside down, a cavalier frog was seeking his fortune. He had heard that a very attractive and rich young lady lived at Greensleeve Manor. So he set out through the wood, intent on finding her and marrying her (and her money).

He came to a road sign that said "Green" something and turned to follow that direction.

When he met the lovely Miss Froggie he did not ask her name, but simply decided that he would marry this beautiful young frog.

He began to court her according to the frog customs of the time.

e gave her tasty gifts of gnats and dragonflies.

He croaked a serenade to her by the light of the moon.

And finally he invited her into the lily pond for a game of leapfrog.

The lady fell in love. She took the dashing cavalier home to meet her parents and to set a wedding date.

But when Mr. Frog saw the simple style of life that his future in-laws enjoyed, he began to wonder if perhaps there was some mistake.

And when he heard his prospective bride and her family talking about sending a wedding invitation to their wealthy neighbors at Greensleeve Manor, he knew he had taken a wrong turn.

That courtship was suddenly over.

And another was about to begin.

Mr. Frog went a-courting, he did ride,
A sword and pistol by his side.

r. Frog retraced his steps and found his way to Greensleeve Manor.

He rode up to Miss Mousie's door,
Where he had never been before.

He set about wooing Miss Mousie without wasting any more time.

He took Miss Mousie on his knee,
Said, "Miss Mouse, will you marry me?"

"My dear Miss Money . . . er . . . Mousie," Mr. Frog croaked, "I have fallen head-over-webfoot in love with you. I want to marry you and share your fortune . . . er, future. Will you (and yours) be mine?"

"You must ask my uncle!" Miss Mousie squeaked.

"Very well, my little furry one," said Mr. Frog. "I hope that your uncle's riches . . . I mean, I hope that your uncle reaches the right decision." The devious frog smiled from ear to ear – as only frogs can do – and a nearby tree rustled angrily for a moment.

Now Uncle Rat when he came home,
Said, "Who's been here since I been gone?"

"A very fine gentleman has been here,
Who wishes me to be his dear."

"You want to marry a FROG?" bellowed Lord Rat. "Whoever heard of such a thing! Why can't you find a nice young vole, or weasel even? At least they're not slippery . . ."

"Mr. Frog is too well-dressed to be slippery!" Miss Mousie protested. "He must be very rich." She showed her uncle Mr. Frog's portrait in the locket he had given her.

Uncle Rat had to admit that Mr. Frog *looked* like a gentleman. And maybe this was his chance to be rid of his extravagant niece.

But something made him uncomfortable. Had Mr. Frog brought more than a marriage proposal to Greensleeve Manor? Uncle Rat couldn't put his paw on it, but something made shivers run down his tail.

Uncle Rat laughed and shook his sides,
To think his niece would be a bride.

Uncle Rat on a horse he went to town,
To buy his niece a wedding gown.

 s he rode into town Lord Rat thought he was really rather lucky to be getting rid of his niece. He set about organizing a wedding that was sure to be the society event of the year.

He ordered the most expensive goods from the most exclusive shops. But he was also intrigued by the market stalls. As he listened to the cries of the stall vendors, he thought he heard his name being bandied about. Was it a frog croaking or a dog barking . . . or both?

Where shall the wedding supper be?
Away down yonder in the hollow tree.

hen the church was booked and the wedding gown ordered, Lord Rat started planning the wedding reception. He'd decided to host a fine supper at the best eating establishment in the land, The Hollow Tree Inn. There the chefs were famous for their "special occasion" banquets, and Lord Rat ordered that his niece's wedding supper was to be the most special occasion of all.

Things were really cooking now.

THE HOLLOW TREE INN

The menu on the illustration reads:

Menu

Cream of Gorgonzola

Warm Surprise
Raised Grub Pie

Beetle Jelly

What shall the wedding supper be?
Three green beans and a black-eyed pea.

The chefs experimented for days with the menu. They found the wedding of a mouse and a frog a particularly amusing challenge. How could they prepare a meal that both bride and groom would enjoy? Should the wedding cake be made of cheese – or mosquitoes?

Everyone was determined to make the wedding of Mr. Frog and Miss Mousie a memorable event.

Tell us what was the bride dressed in?
A cream gauze veil and a brass breastpin.

Tell us what was the groom dressed in?
Sky blue breeches with silver stitches.

inally the wedding day dawned. St. Whisker's church was full of squeaking. Mr. Frog thought he looked very fine in his new breeches from the fashionable shop, "Frogs' Legs." He was still looking at himself in the mirror when he heard the parson's words:

". . . and wilt thou, Mr. Frog, take this mouse to be thy wedded wife, to live together in matrimony?"
"What? Money? . . . I mean matrimony? Yes, of course I shall!"

"If any of you know cause, or just impediment why these two animals should not be joined together in matrimony, declare it now."

Mr. Frog thought he heard an angry croak, but then thought perhaps it was only his conscience speaking.

No one else heard it, and so the frog and mouse were pronounced husband and wife.

19

t was the wedding of the year. Everyone kissed the bride, congratulated the groom, and proceeded to The Hollow Tree Inn, where Lord Rat had organized music and dancing.

Mr. Frog and Miss Mousie refreshed themselves with glasses of fruit fly punch, then took to the dance floor when the musicians arrived.

First to come in was a bumblebee,
To play the fiddle upon his knee.

Mr. Frog found he had developed a taste for music.

Lord Rat was very pleased. It seemed that all of polite society was at his party, dancing to his tune.

What went on outside was not yet of interest to him.

Next to come in was a little black tick,
Ate so much it made him sick.

Next to come in was Dr. Fly,
Said Mr. Tick would surely die.

Who then came into the room,
Asked to see the bride and groom?

hen a stranger appeared at the door, the dormouse on guard demanded to see her invitation.

"What! Don't you know who I am, you scruffy rodent?" The huge creature lurched into the Inn as if pushed by an outside force.

The dormouse had never seen such a big mouse before, but he thought perhaps this was one of the rodents from Uncle Rat's side of the family. Certainly she was rich, possibly she was royal.

He bowed low and stepped aside.

n a flash, before you could say "disguise," the giant mouse had removed her nose and whiskers and picked up a knife and fork.

The wedding party stood frozen in disbelief.

Fur everywhere stood on end as the stranger hobbled toward the wedding cake.

"Good afternoon," purred the pussycat. "Now how about playing one of my favorite party games? It's called 'Cat and Mouse . . . and Rat and Frog!'"
The cat meowed and sprang forward singing,

"Away down yonder in the hollow tree,
Who *shall the wedding supper be?*

I'm the famous big gray cat,
Who fancies a dinner of mouse and rat!"

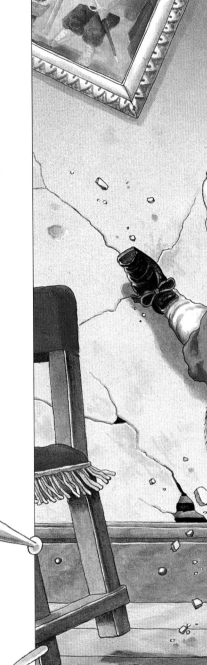

24

He helped himself to the wedding cake,
Then chased the party down to the lake.

r. Frog ran to the window as fast as his fancy blue breeches would let him.

Miss Mousie thought that this was not the most elegant way for a bride to take leave of her wedding reception, but picked up her skirts and scampered after the groom.

Lord Rat hated to leave his supper behind, but on balance thought he'd rather leave it than *be* it.

With a hop, a squeak, and a croak, the wedding party ran to the water's edge where a boat was waiting to take the bride and groom on their honeymoon.

How fortunate Lord Rat had decided on a boat rather than any other means of transportation! At least the cat would not be able to catch them now.

They leaped aboard and breathed a sigh of relief. But soon they noticed something odd. Their paws were wet – and getting wetter.

" shall demand my money back," exclaimed Lord Rat as the boat began to sink.

But then they noticed another odd thing. It had suddenly gotten very dark – and it was getting darker. The three looked up, and a huge pair of eyes looked down at them. The eyes belonged to a big, black . . .

"SNAKE!" screamed the frog, the rat, and the mouse.

"sSSUPPER!" hissed the snake, flicking a long, forked tongue.

They all went sailing across the lake,
And they all were swallowed by a big
black snake.

And there's the end of one, two, three,
The rat, the frog, and Miss Mousie!

And now begins another tale,
Of the other frog, a young female,

Who took revenge on Mr. Frog.
Will she now marry Captain Dog

There's bread and cheese upon the shelf.
If you want any more you can sing it yourself!

A DORLING KINDERSLEY BOOK

Mr. Frog went a-courting, he did ride,
A sword and pistol by his side.

He took Miss Mousie on his knee,
Said, "Miss Mouse, will you marry me?"

First American Edition, 1994
2 4 6 8 10 9 7 5 3 1

Published in the United States by Dorling Kindersley Publishing, Inc.,
95 Madison Avenue, New York, New York 10016

Library of Congress Cataloging-in-Publication Data
Chalk, Gary.
Mr. Frog went a-courting / written and illustrated by Gary Chalk.
—1st American ed.
p.   cm.
Summary: Illustrations and supplementary text elaborate on the story
of the wedding of a frog and a mouse in a traditional folk song.
ISBN 1-56458-622-7
1. Folk songs, English—Texts. [1. Folk songs.] I. Title.
PZ8.3.C355Mr   1994
782.42162'21—dc20   94-9560
                                                 CIP
                                                 AC

Color reproduction by DOT Gradations Ltd.
Printed and bound in Great Britain by BPC Paulton Books, Bristol.